GOOD GUYS

5-MINUTE STORIES

10 BOOKS IN 1!

Houghton Mifflin Harcourt

Boston New York

CONTENTS

ONE HOT SUMMER DAY, JAMES WENT ON A
LONG DRIVE TO BILL AND PAM'S HOUSE SO HE COULD GO TO
A WEEK OF NATURE CAMP WITH HIS FRIEND EAMON.
BILL AND PAM ARE EAMON'S GRANDPARENTS.
THEY LIVE AT THE BEACH.

EAMON WAS ALREADY THERE.

NATURE CAMP WAS BILL'S IDEA.
BILL LOVED NATURE — ESPECIALLY COLD, WILD, AND
REMOTE PLACES WITH HARDLY ANY PEOPLE.
HE HAD BEEN TO MANY OF THESE SORTS OF PLACES BEFORE.
BUT THE PLACE HE MOST WANTED TO VISIT WAS ANTARCTICA
(BECAUSE OF THE PENGUINS).
PAM SAID SHE PREFERRED PEOPLE OVER PENGUINS.

EAMON THOUGHT THIS CHAT
WAS FASCINATING.
BUT HE HOPED JAMES
WOULD ARRIVE SOON.

DING DONG!

AND FINALLY, JAMES DID...

WITH JUST A COUPLE

OF HIS BELONGINGS.

HE HAD NEVER BEEN AWAY FROM HOME FOR AN ENTIRE WEEK,
SO HE WAS VERY SAD WHEN HIS MOTHER DROVE AWAY.

THE FIRST THING BILL WANTED TO DO BEFORE NATURE CAMP STARTED
WAS TO TAKE JAMES AND EAMON TO THE PENGUIN EXHIBIT AT THE
NATURAL HISTORY MUSEUM.
PAM OFFERED TO PACK A PICNIC OF PEANUT BUTTER-AND-HONEY SANDWICHES.
JAMES AND EAMON DISCUSSED THEIR OPTIONS.

THEY DECIDED TO STAY HOME AND ENJOY
BILL AND PAM'S COMPANY.

IN THE MORNING, BILL TOOK THE BOYS
TO NATURE CAMP.
THE ROAD WAS LONG AND CURVY.
JAMES AND EAMON LEARNED
A LOT OF NEW VOCABULARY WORDS
WHILE BILL DROVE.

ON THE WAY BACK THAT AFTERNOON, JAMES AND EAMON
DESCRIBED THEIR FIRST NATURE CAMP DAY TO BILL.

WHEN THEY GOT HOME, BILL UNROLLED A LARGE MAP OF ANTARCTICA ON THE LIVING-ROOM FLOOR.

PAM GAVE JAMES AND EAMON COFFEE ICE-CREAM ICEBERGS WITH HARD CHOCOLATE SAUCE ON TOP.

NATURE CAMP MADE THE BOYS VERY HUNGRY.

BILL BROUGHT TIDE CHARTS AND A GLOBE TO THE DINNER TABLE.
PAM SERVED BANANA WAFFLES WITH MAPLE SYRUP.

AT NIGHT, JAMES AND EAMON SLEPT
ON A BLOW-UP MATTRESS
WITH AN AUTOMATIC PUMP.

BILL AND PAM WONDERED IF THEY WOULD BE LONELY IN THE DOWNSTAIRS BEDROOM,

BUT THEY WEREN'T.

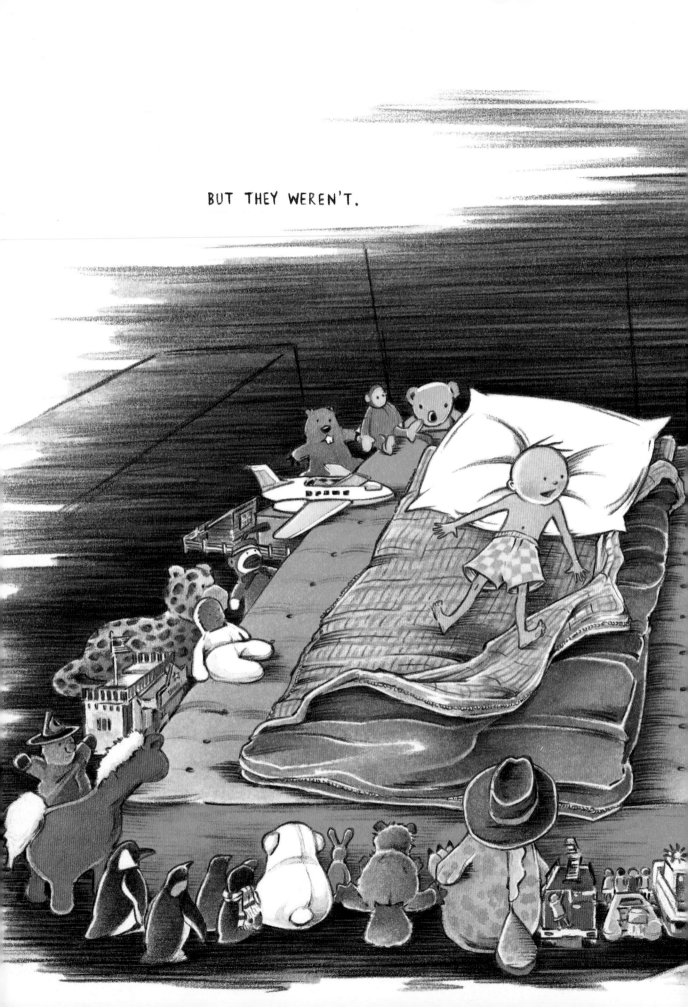

BEFORE THEY LEFT FOR NATURE CAMP THE NEXT MORNING,
BILL HANDED THEM EACH A PAIR OF BINOCULARS
AND A LIST OF BIRDS TO LOOK FOR.
ON THE WAY HOME, THE BOYS REPORTED THEIR FINDINGS.

AS THE NATURE CAMP WEEK
WENT BY, JAMES AND EAMON
PRACTICALLY BECAME ONE PERSON.
THEY DID EVERYTHING TOGETHER IN EXACTLY THE SAME WAY.
TO SAVE TIME, BILL BEGAN CALLING THEM JAMON.
HE WOULD SAY, "HEY JAMON, THINK ABOUT
WHETHER OR NOT YOU WANT TO SEE
THAT PENGUIN EXHIBIT."

AND JAMON WOULD THINK ABOUT IT.

THEN IN COMPLETE AGREEMENT, THE CAMPERS WOULD DECIDE
TO PRACTICE QUIET MEDITATION DOWNSTAIRS,

EAT MORE
BANANA WAFFLES,

AND ENJOY THE BEACH TOGETHER....

NATURE CAMP WAS JUST SO GREAT.

AND THEN ON FRIDAY AFTERNOON, NATURE CAMP WAS OVER.
JAMES AND EAMON RECAPPED THE WEEK DURING THE DRIVE HOME.

ON THEIR LAST NIGHT TOGETHER,
BILL, PAM, JAMES, AND EAMON HAD A POPCORN PARTY.
JAMES AND EAMON SOON DISCOVERED THAT A PARTY WITH
BILL AND PAM COULD GET PRETTY NOISY.

SO, THEY WANDERED OUTSIDE
FOR SOME PEACE AND QUIET.
TOMORROW THEY HAD TO GO HOME.

THEY LOOKED UP AT THE SKY AND OUT AT THE OCEAN.

FOR THE FIRST TIME ALL WEEK,

THEY COULDN'T THINK OF ANYTHING TO DO.

THE SUN WENT DOWN.

THE STARS CAME OUT.

THEN AT LAST, JAMES AND EAMON

FINALLY GOT REAL BUSY WITH SOMETHING...

AND IT TURNED OUT TO BE THE VERY BEST PART OF THE BEST WEEK EVER.

IN THE MORNING, JAMES AND EAMON COULDN'T WAIT
TO SHOW BILL AND PAM WHAT THEY HAD MADE.

BILL GAVE THE BOYS A BIG HUG.
HE SAID THIS WAS HOW PENGUINS HUDDLE TOGETHER
TO KEEP WARM.

PAM SAID SHE PREFERRED PEOPLE HUGS
OVER PENGUIN HUDDLES.

JAMES AND EAMON HUGGED
BILL AND PAM BACK
(SORT OF).

AND WHEN THEIR MOMS
FINALLY ARRIVED TO TAKE THEM HOME,
JAMES AND EAMON GAVE EACH OTHER THE

SECRET JAMON HANDSHAKE...

AND THEN THEY WALKED LIKE A COUPLE OF PENGUINS
ALL THE WAY OUT THE FRONT DOOR.

The moon shined brightly as Nicholas readied for bed.
This is what he could hear:

his baby sister crying in her crib,

the dog barking to be let out,

and the radio blaring on the front porch.

Even the noises from his neighborhood floated through his open window.
Too loud, thought Nicholas, holding his ears, *and I'm NOT going to bed!*
In that moment, Nicholas made a decision.

He tiptoed quietly to the kitchen.
He packed two cheese and tomato sandwiches,
one bottle of water, a bunch of grapes, and a cookie.
He fit the food nicely into his lunch box along with a napkin.

Next, Nicholas got dressed. First he climbed into his space suit.
Then he put on his space boots. At last he put on his space helmet.
Nicholas read his list aloud to make sure he was ready.

Then Nicholas walked outside to the backyard and climbed into his rocket.

He strapped himself in and prepared for takeoff.
Nicholas knew exactly which buttons to push, and when to push them.
"Four . . . three . . . two . . . one . . . liftoff!"
he shouted. The rocket soared into space.

Nicholas turned and looked out the window.

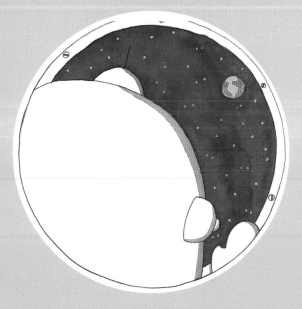

Below, he could see the noisy world slowly fall away.

Above, he saw the moon.

Almost there, he thought.

The rocket touched down gently on the lunar surface.
Nicholas opened the hatch, climbed down the ladder,
and stepped onto the cold, dusty landscape.

It was *so* quiet on the moon.

This is what Nicholas could *not* hear:
his baby sister crying,
the dog barking,
or the radio blaring.

How nice, thought Nicholas.
He spread out his blanket and unpacked his snack.

The lack of gravity was a problem. The tomato slices rose softly into the atmosphere.

They looked as big and round as the earth as they slowly floated away.

Nicholas held on to his sandwich and ate what was left.
He ate his grapes, took a sip of water, and saved his cookie for last.
"Delicious!" he said to himself.

When he had finished, Nicholas went for a moonwalk.
He bounded across huge craters and scaled miniature mountains.
The beautiful blue earth appeared behind every peak, silent and peaceful.

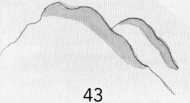

As Nicholas walked, he looked back at his
footprints in the soft lunar surface. *Just like
footprints at the beach,* he thought, remembering how
he had helped his baby sister take her very first steps toward
the ocean in the cool wet sand.

Nicholas continued his walk. The vast, wide-open spaces on the moon
reminded him of his dog.

Wouldn't he just love to run and run and run, with no end in sight?
Nicholas thought. *Though he would probably miss the green grass in our yard.*

And seeing the earth again, Nicholas remembered those warm summer nights when his family sat out on the porch in the light of the full moon.

This moon.

His moonwalk had brought him back to his spaceship.
Back up the ladder went Nicholas. He climbed
through the hatch and strapped himself in.
"Four . . . three . . . two . . . one . . . liftoff!" he shouted.

The rocket soared into space. Nicholas could see the craters and valleys of the silent moon slowly fall away.

Ahead, he saw the earth.

Soon the rocket touched down gently in his backyard. Nicholas opened the hatch, climbed down the ladder, and stepped onto the moonlit grass.

He went into his room and took off his space suit, his space helmet, and his space boots. He tiptoed gently down the hallway.

This is what Nicholas could see:

his baby sister sleeping in her crib,

the dog curled snugly in his bed, and

his parents sitting together on the porch, listening to the radio.

It was a lovely evening in his neighborhood.

beep! beep!   vroom! vroom!

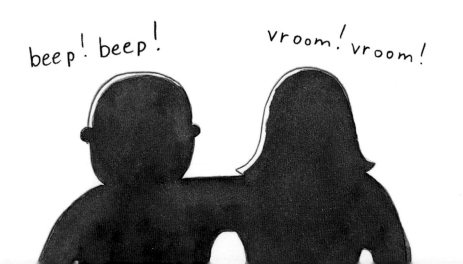

"I'm ready for bed now," Nicholas told his parents. "Good night."

"Good night, Nicholas," said his parents.

It was good to be home.

There is a
big fish tank
in the window,

Friday is my favorite day.
On Fridays I have dinner
with Grandpa Sam.
He owns a restaurant
in Chinatown.

and everyone
stops to look.

"Hi, Louie!" says Dan the waiter
when we come in.
Everyone is very busy eating.

EXIT

In the kitchen
I say hello to Chef Ben.
There is so much steam,
I can hardly see him.
"Hi, Louie—is that you?" he says.

David is busy
rolling egg rolls.

I like to watch Chef Lee
chop vegetables.
His hands move so fast.

Liang is peeling shrimp.

Suddenly Jai rushes in. "Delivery pickup!"
He takes the bags and puts them on his bicycle
and then rides away.
"He even delivers in the pouring rain!" Liang says.

"Where are the spareribs
 for table eight?"
calls Dan from the door.
"They're on their way!" another waiter shouts back.

"Time to eat," Grandpa Sam says.
"I'm hungry."

"Me too," I say.

We sit at a table under the paper dragon,
which Grandpa says brings good luck.

I see my friend.
"Hey, Franklin!" I say.

"This is my favorite food,"
 he tells me.
"Cool!" I say. "Me too!"

My grandpa and I eat with chopsticks, but most of the time at home I use a fork, knife, and spoon.

The waiter brings a big bowl of rice.
He brings steamed dumplings, egg rolls,
and shrimp chow mein.
My favorite.

The waiter brings crabs.

"I don't think so!"

Grandpa orders a fish.

"No, thank you, Grandpa!"

At the end of dinner,
Grandpa gives me
a fortune cookie.
I open it up and
Grandpa reads,
"Happy food,
happy belly,
happy smile."

Then the waiter puts
a dish of orange slices
on the table.
I go over to Franklin,
and he turns around.

Grandpa laughs.
"Now, that's what
I call a happy smile!"

GUYKU

A Year of Haiku for Boys

WRITTEN BY **BOB RACZKA** ART BY **PETER H. REYNOLDS**

Spring

The wind and I play
tug-of-war with my new kite.
The wind is winning.

I free grasshopper
from his tight, ten-fingered cage —
he tickles too much!

With baseball cards and
clothespins, we make our bikes sound
like motorcycles.

In a rushing stream,
we turn rocks into a dam.
Hours flow by us.

If this puddle could talk, I think it would tell me to splash my sister.

I watch the worms squirm and decide to bait my hook with hot dog instead.

Summer

Pine tree invites me
to climb him up to the sky.
How can I refuse?

Mosquito lands on
my cheek. I try to slap her,
but I just slap me.

Lying on the lawn,
we study the blackboard sky.
Connecting the dots.

Skip, skip, skip, skip, plunk!
Five ripple rings in a row —
my best throw ever!

Penny on the rail,
you used to look like Lincoln
before you got smooshed.

With the ember end
of my long marshmallow stick,
I draw on the dark.

Fall

Hey, who turned off all the crickets? I'm not ready for summer to end.

We follow deer tracks
in the mud, pretending that
we too are wild beasts.

Helicopters spin
in squadrons from our maple—
I almost caught one!

The best part about
kicking this stone home from school
is there are no rules.

From underneath the
leaf pile, my invisible
brother is giggling.

Pounding fat cattails
on a park bench near the pond,
We make a snowstorm.

Winter

Winter must be here.
Every time I open my
mouth, a cloud comes out.

How many million
flakes will it take to make a
snow day tomorrow?

Two splotches of white
on a black tree trunk. I aim
my next pitch—*strike three!*

Icicles dangle,
begging to be broken off
for a short sword fight.

It's silent under
these pine boughs sagging with snow,
like hibernating.

Last week's snowman looks
under the weather. Must be
a spring allergy.

MUSTACHE BABY

Bridget Heos

Illustrations by Joy Ang

When Baby Billy was born,
his family noticed something odd:

He had a

mustache.

"What does this mean?" his mother asked.

"Well, it depends," the nurse said.
"You'll have to wait and see whether
it is a good-guy mustache or a
bad-guy mustache."

At first, it was plain to see that Billy's mustache was noble and just. He tamed a bucking bronco and became a **COWBOY**.

He always protected his cattle . . .

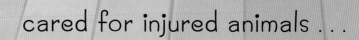

cared for injured animals . . .

and mended broken fences.

After setting things right on the range, Billy rode off to become:

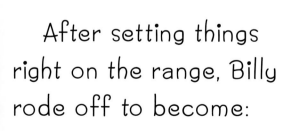

A SPANISH PAINTER.

A ringleader.

A SWORD FIGHTER.

And finally . . .

a **MAN OF THE LAW**,

for his neighborhood desperately needed him.

With his cop badge, Billy was one tough hombre.

He stopped speeders . . .

outlawed poker . . .

and caught thieves red-handed.

Everyone loved having Officer Billy around.

But a funny thing happened.
As Billy got bigger . . .

his mustache grew and curled up
at the ends.

His parents' worst fears were
realized. Billy had a . . .

BAD-GUY
mustache.

Billy's disreputable mustache
led him into a life of dreadful crime.
He became:

A cat burglar.

A CEREAL CRIMINAL.

And a **TRAIN ROBBER** so heartless
that he even stole the tracks.

But when he planned the biggest
heist of all—a bank robbery—

his getaway car wasn't fast enough.

He got caught . . .

and thrown in jail.

Jail is no place for a baby.
Even a baby with a mustache.

Billy tried to be strong, but
he did shed a few tears.

After ages and ages, Billy regretted his treacherous thievery. He wished that his evil mustache would go away.

At last,
his mother busted him out of jail.

"There, there," she said.
"Everybody has a bad-mustache
day now and then."

"Let's dry your tears," his
father said. "The new neighbors
have a baby your age. He's
coming over to play."

DING-DONG

TAMMI SAUER   ILLUSTRATED BY ARTHUR HOWARD

QuieT WYatT

SUPER SHY—
OR SUPERHERO?

Wyatt liked quiet.
And being quiet worked for Wyatt.
He was a spectacular tree
in the school play.

He was the model visitor at the dinosaur museum.

QUIET
PLEASE

He was a total star at ninja camp.

Wyatt's world was
perfectly quiet . . .

. . . until his class went on a field trip and he was paired with Noreen. Noreen was anything but quiet.

"I'm the *queen* of nature," said Noreen. "Let's do this, field trip buddy!" Wyatt gulped. Quietly, of course.

"Fishing is my specialty," said Noreen.
"This is how to cast a line."

Wyatt gaped. Quietly, of course.

"I was born for boating," said Noreen.
"This is how to paddle a canoe."

Wyatt dripped. Quietly, of course.

"Wow," said Noreen. "I'm so good at noticing the details, it's scary."

It was a very busy field trip.

There was bird-watching.

"Binoculars are for beginners, Wyatt."

There was hiking.

"This is what you call trailblazing, Wyatt."

There was ziplining.
"Don't look down, Wyatt!"

Somebody got *extra* quiet.

When it was time to return to the bus,
Noreen had lots to say.
"Nature's not *all* I'm good at.
There's math and cartwheels and . . .
Oops! Almost forgot.
I have the gift of song."

La
La La
La
La La
La

One thing was clear.

For the first time in the history of Wyatt,

he could not stay quiet.

La La La La La

"NOREEN! ROCKS!"

"Thanks," said Noreen.
"Glad you think so!"

Then . . .

"Uh-oh," said Noreen.

Everyone was wowed.

Especially Noreen.

"I'm an excellent ninja," said Wyatt.

"Good to know, field trip buddy," said Noreen.

The bus headed back to school.
"Hey, Mr. Driver," said Noreen.
"I know a shortcut!"

Wyatt didn't know *what* to say.
So he stayed quiet.

But, from time to time,
Wyatt wasn't so quiet.

"See?" said Wyatt.

"*Oh,*" said Noreen.
Wyatt smiled. Quietly, of course.
He still liked quiet.

He also liked having a friend.

KID AMAZING

vs. THE BLOB

Josh Schneider

Theodor Seuss Geisel Award Winner

AAAAAAAAAAA

ONE DAY, while practicing his letters, Jimmy is interrupted by an extremely annoying howl. And, right on cue, there's the emergency catastrophe alarm! Jimmy rushes to the closet. He touches the tennis racket like *this* and pulls the light string like *so* and—*whoosh!*—a secret door opens.

Jimmy goes through the secret door and into a secret elevator.
The secret elevator takes him down and down until he reaches a
secret base, where—

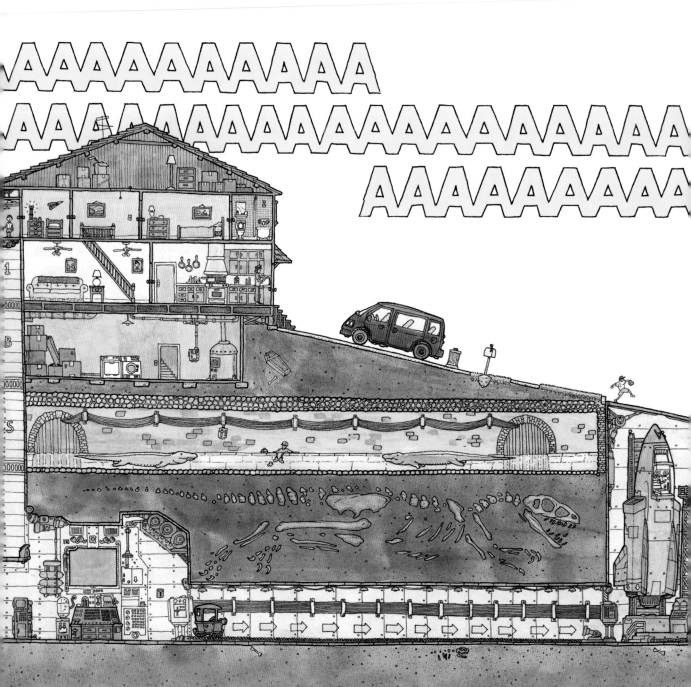

Kerzing!

Jimmy is transformed into Kid Amazing!

KID AMAZING GADGET

#27
Footie Pajamas

These striking all-terrain pajamas are the perfect suit for our hard-working superhero, protecting him from everything a villain might throw at him. The very, very sweaty feet are a small price to pay.

KID AMAZING GADGET

#55
Mystery Cloth

The origin of this mystery cloth is unknown (although it does bear a slight resemblance to a missing black tie). In any event, with the Kid's brilliant addition of two holes, it now keeps his secret identity safe.

KID AMAZING GADGET

#128
Dishwashing Gloves

When Kid Amazing rolls up his sleeves to take care of evil, these rare red dishwashing gloves are there to shield his mighty hands from lava, ice, lasers, acid, toxic goo, and pruny-ness.

KID AMAZING GADGET

#86
Baseball Cap

When duty calls, the cap of Jimmy, humble right fielder for Big Al's Automotive Little League team, becomes the cap of Kid Amazing, vanquisher of villainy and star pitcher for the Galactic Hero Little League team.

It's the Commissioner.

"What is it, Commissioner?" asks Kid Amazing.

"Jimmy—" says the Commissioner.

"Kid Amazing," says Kid Amazing.

"Kid Amazing," says the Commissioner. "Do you hear that howling? Could you please see what's going on?"

"I'm on it," says Kid Amazing. Who could it be?
An evil giant robot? Those space lobsters again?
No, only one thing could howl such an annoying howl:
Kid Amazing's arch-nemesis, the Blob!

"The Blob!" says Kid Amazing. "Don't worry. I'll take care of *her*."

Kid Amazing uses his robo-sniffer to catch the Blob's terrible scent. The stink trail leads right to the Blob's lair.

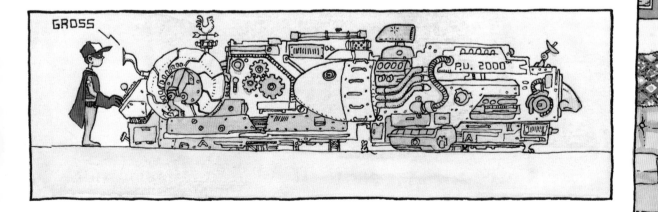

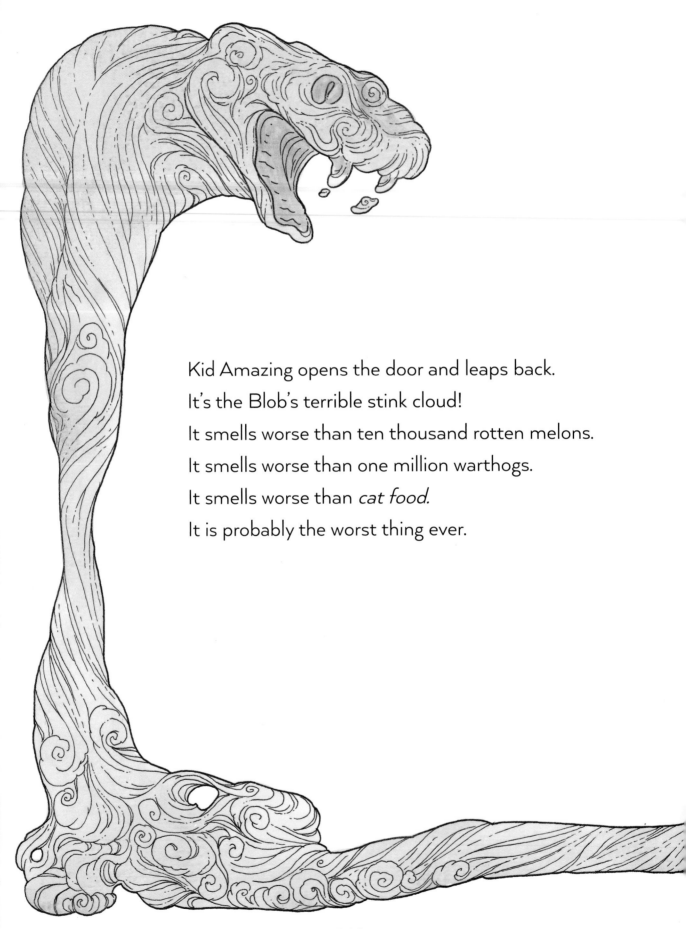

Kid Amazing opens the door and leaps back.

It's the Blob's terrible stink cloud!

It smells worse than ten thousand rotten melons.

It smells worse than one million warthogs.

It smells worse than *cat food.*

It is probably the worst thing ever.

KID AMAZING GADGET

#157

Eau de Pommes Frites

Kid Amazing got it for the Commissioner for her birthday, but she doesn't use it for some reason, so it's been added to the arsenal.

Kid Amazing quick-thinkingly grabs his de-stinking spray from his utility belt, and—*spritz!* So much for *that* stink cloud.

Entering the Blob's lair,
Kid Amazing slips and slides
on the slime-covered floor.

The Blob must be close.

But to reach her, he must clear a safe, slip-free path. Kid Amazing reaches for his de-sliming wipe and—*fwip!*—the lair is dry.

And there on her throne is the Blob.

She is howling a terrible, annoying howl.

Kid Amazing reaches for his utility belt, but it's empty!

He is out of de-stinking spray.

He is out of de-sliming wipes.

What will Kid Amazing do?

The howl is melting his brain. He dives for cover.

Then he sees it: the Blob's howl neutralizer.

Kid Amazing grabs the neutralizer and—*pop!*—the Blob stops howling.

Kid Amazing has saved the day.

"I have saved the day," says Kid Amazing. "Also, the Blob needs a new stink-containment unit."

"Thanks," says the Commissioner. "But please stop calling your sister the Blob."

"No thanks necessary," says Kid Amazing. "Saving the day is its own reward. Although a cookie is also a very good reward."

"I'll see what I can do," says the Commissioner.

"Another happy ending for the forces of justice," says Kid Amazing. "That's the last trouble we'll get from *her.*"

Brothers

David McPhail

Author and illustrator of *Sisters*

This is the story of two brothers.

Most of the time they get along . . .

but not always.

Sometimes they squabble . . .

like when they both want
to ride the same bike.

So then they take turns.

Sometimes they disagree about whose
turn it is to walk the dog . . .

so they walk the
dog together.

Brothers can share
the blame.

And they take care
of each other.
When one hurts his knee . . .

the other pulls him
home in the wagon.

Brothers can be both alike and different.

They both like to wear soccer jerseys . . .

but one likes to wear his inside out!

They both like
chocolate ice cream.
But one likes his in a cone . . .

while the other insists
on a cup and spoon.

One brother can tie his shoes.
The other one . . . not so much.

But he doesn't mind.

Both brothers like to splash in puddles.
One likes to wear his coat, hat, and boots . . .

while the other likes to
wear nothing at all!

Too bright!

At bedtime, one brother likes
the window shade up.

The other likes the window
shade down.

So they leave it halfway.

If there is thunder
in the night . . .

the brothers get under one bed
until the storm passes.

And they know, those brothers do,
that they will stick together . . .

always.

MARGRET & H.A. REY'S

Curious George

and the Firefighters

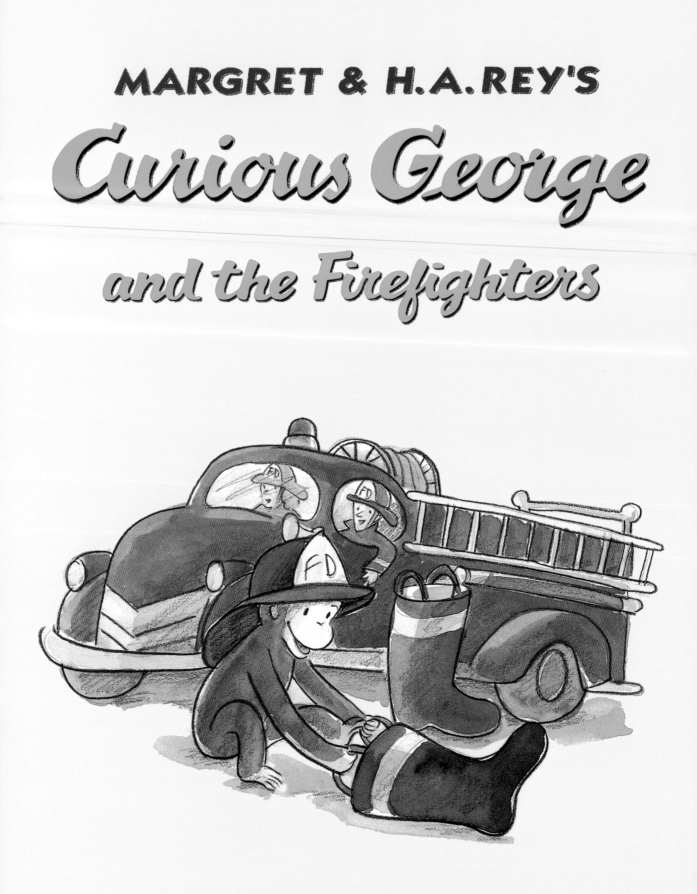

This is George.

He was a good little monkey and always very curious.

Today George and the man with the yellow hat

joined Mrs. Gray's class on their field trip to the fire station.

"Welcome!" the Fire Chief said, and he led everyone upstairs to begin their tour. He told them all about being a firefighter. George tried to pay attention, but there were so many things to explore.

Like where did that pole go? George was curious.

Why, it went back downstairs to the big fire truck! There was a map of the city and a whole wall of uniforms!

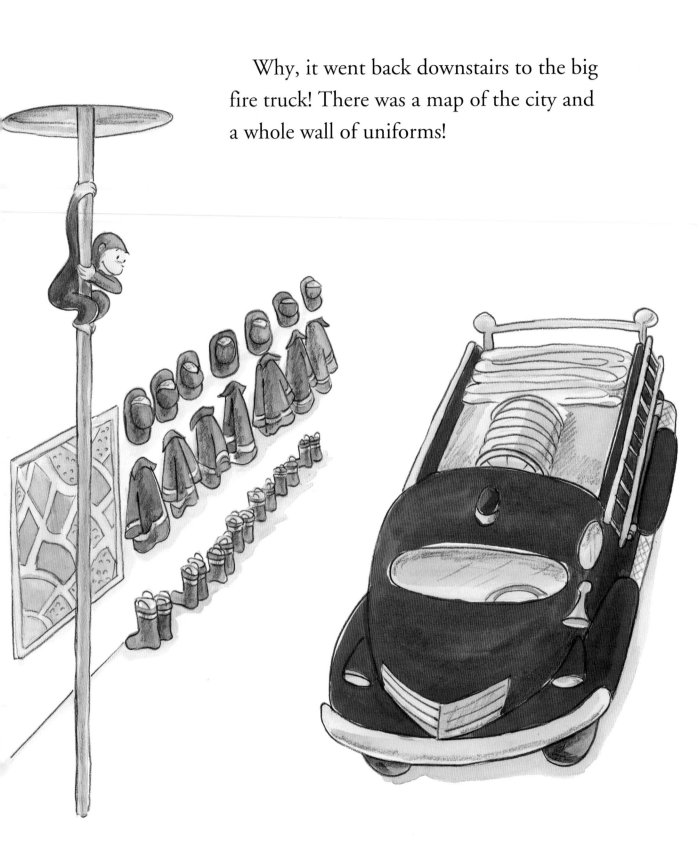

George had an idea.
First, he stepped into a
pair of boots.

Next, he picked out a helmet.

And, finally, George put on a jacket.
He was a firefighter!

Suddenly . . . BRRRIINNGG!

The firefighters all rushed in.

"This is not my helmet!" said one.

"My boots are too big!" said another.

"Hurry! Hurry!" called the Fire Chief. There was no time to waste!

One by one, the firefighters jumped into the fire truck.

And so did George.

With lights flashing, the fire truck with all the firefighters and George sped out of the firehouse.

The truck turned right. Then it turned left. "WHOO WHOO WHOO," went the whistle and George held on tight.

Quickly the fire truck and all the firefighters pulled up to a pizza parlor. Smoke was coming out of a window and a crowd gathered in the street.

"Thank goodness you're here!" cried the cook.

The firefighters started unwinding their hoses. They knew just what to do.

And George was ready to help.

One of the firefighters saw George trying to help,
and he led him out of the way.

"A fire is no place for a monkey!" he said to George.
"You stay here where it's safe."

George felt terrible.

George sat on the bench and saw
a bucket full of balls. George
reached in and took one out.

A little girl was watching George. He tried to
give her the ball, but she was too frightened.

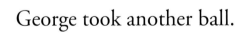

George took another ball.

And another.
"Look," a boy said.
"That monkey is juggling!"

The boy found a ball and tossed it
to George, but it went too high.

George climbed up onto
the fire truck to get it and

George showed them
his juggling tricks!

The boy threw another ball
to George, and George tossed it
back. The little girl picked up a
ball, too. Soon all the children
were playing catch.

The Fire Chief told everyone that the fire was out. Just then, the little girl laughed and said, "Look, Mommy—a fire monkey!"

"Hey!" called the Fire Chief. "What are you doing up there?"

"What a good idea," the little girl's mother said to the Fire Chief. "Bringing this brave little monkey to help children when they're scared."

"Oh," the Fire Chief said. "Well, er, thank you."

Before long the fire truck was back at the fire house. "George!" called the man with the yellow hat.

"Is everyone all right?" asked Mrs. Gray.

"Yes, it was just a small fire," said the Fire Chief. "And George was a big help." The field trip was coming to an end, and there was one thing left to do. . .

All the children got to take a ride around the neighborhood on the shiny red fire truck, and they each got their very own fire helmet. Even George! And it was just the right size for a brave little monkey.

REAL COWBOYS

Kate Hoefler   illustrated by Jonathan Bean

Real cowboys are quiet in the morning, careful not to wake the people who live in little houses in the hollow, and up the mountains, and at the edge of fields in the distance.

Their work is to think of others: of the calf stranded on the ridge, and their dog coaxing it down—of how hundreds of moving cattle will feel about the sound of distant thunder.

Real cowboys are gentle. They know all the songs that keep cattle calm, moving out of storms, along dirt roads and narrow canyons.

At night, they sing lullabies over the calls
of coyotes—songs that keep cows
on a prairie deep in sleep.

They head to places called Stillwater or Red Town, but wherever they are, real cowboys are good listeners. They're always listening to their trail boss and to the other cowhands.

Sometimes they listen for trucks, and wolves, and rushing water. And sometimes they just listen to the big wide world and its grass song.

Real cowboys are safe. They pull their hats low because the sun can burn, and wear chaps so the cacti and brush don't cut them.

They're on cattle drives for hours, or days, or weeks, but they don't mind. Real cowboys are patient.

Even on a fast horse, they have to move with the slow rhythm of a herd, and it can take a long time to get places.

Real cowboys ask for help.
They use hand and hat signals
to let others know they need them,
and they ask their dogs for help too.
Real cowboys are good to their dogs.
They have a special way of talking to them.
Cowboys say "Go by" and "Look back,"
and their dogs listen, driving in a lost heifer.

Real cowboys want peace.
They don't want stampedes, where all the cattle
spook, and thunder over the earth,
and scatter in dust storms.

But sometimes it happens.

Some of those cattle and dogs are never found, and cowboys think of them from time to time when everything else on the prairie is quiet.

Real cowboys cry.

Real cowboys take turns. They make camp when the sun is as low as sagebrush, and eat in twos and threes at the chuck wagon. Later, they take turns watching over the cattle while others stretch out under mesquite moons.

Real cowboys are good to the earth.
They pick up their campsites, and keep
cattle moving to save water and grasslands.

Real cowboys can be strong, and tough,
and homesick at the same time.
They imagine the faces of people they love
in the mountains they pass.

Real cowboys are as many different colors as the earth.

Real cowboys are girls, too.

Real cowboys are artists. They create. They dream. They make up stories for their friends, and horses, and dogs—stories about the world that are bigger than moving cattle to Stillwater or Red Town.

They sit under skies so big, the stars take shape on the ground, and they wonder what's past the horizon.

And one day, when their work is done,
real cowboys find out.